my itty-bitty bio

Susan B. Anthony

Published in the United States of America by Cherry Lake Publishing
Ann Arbor, Michigan
www.cherrylakepublishing.com

Reading Adviser: Marla Conn, MS, Ed, Literacy Specialist, Read-Ability, Inc.
Book Designer: Jennifer Wahi
Illustrator: Jeff Bane

Photo Credits: © LEE SNIDER PHOTO IMAGES/Shutterstock.com, 5; © Everett Historical/Shutterstock.com, 7, 13, 17, 19, 21, 23; ©Library of Congress/Reproduction No. LC-USZ62-123257, 9; © Library of Congress/Reproduction No. LC-USZ61-791, 11; © Wikimedia, 15, 22; Cover, 1, 6, 12, 18, Jeff Bane; Various frames throughout, ©Shutterstock Images

Library of Congress Cataloging-in-Publication Data

Names: Spiller, Sara author. | Bane, Jeff, 1957- illustrator.
Title: Susan B. Anthony / by Sara Spiller ; illustrated by Jeff Bane.
Description: Ann Arbor, Michigan : Cherry Lake Publishing, 2019. | Series: My itty-bitty bio | Includes bibliographical references and index.
Identifiers: LCCN 2018034506| ISBN 9781534142671 (hardcover) | ISBN 9781534140431 (pdf) | ISBN 9781534139237 (pbk.) | ISBN 9781534141636 (hosted ebook)
Subjects: LCSH: Anthony, Susan B. (Susan Brownell), 1820-1906--Juvenile literature. | Suffragists--United States--Biography--Juvenile literature. | Feminists--United States--Biography--Juvenile literature. | Women's rights--United States--Juvenile literature.
Classification: LCC HQ1413.A55 S65 2019 | DDC 305.42092 [B] --dc23
LC record available at https://lccn.loc.gov/2018034506

Printed in the United States of America
Corporate Graphics

table of contents

About the author: Sara Spiller is a native of the state of Michigan. She enjoys reading comic books and hanging out with her cats.

About the illustrator: Jeff Bane and his two business partners own a studio along the American River in Folsom, California, home of the 1849 Gold Rush. When Jeff's not sketching or illustrating for clients, he's either swimming or kayaking in the river to relax.

my story

I was born in Massachusetts in 1820. I grew up in a **Quaker** family. We helped with social problems.

1817
SUSAN B. ANTHONY

I worked as a teacher.
I worked to end **slavery**.
I was an **abolitionist**.

I also wanted to
ban **alcohol**.

What would you ban? Why?

I wanted to talk to people about banning alcohol. But I was not allowed. Men did not listen to women's ideas.

I met Elizabeth Cady Stanton in 1851. We were at an antislavery meeting. We began working together. We shared our ideas with others.

How do you make friends?

After slavery ended, we worked for women's rights. I wanted women to **vote**. I wanted women to be allowed to own land.

SUSAN B. ANTHONY
NATIONAL AMERICAN WOMAN SUFFRAGE ASSOCIATION
FOUNDED IN 1869
SUPPORTS BRISTOW-MONDELL RESOLUTION
DRAFTED BY SUSAN B. ANTHONY, 1874
FIRST, LAST AND ALWAYS
1874
1914

I traveled more. We started groups that wanted women's rights.

In 1872, I voted. This was not allowed.

I was **arrested** for voting. I was told to pay money. I didn't do anything wrong. I never paid.

When have you disagreed with a rule?

Later I met President Theodore Roosevelt. I got him thinking about supporting women's right to vote.

I died in 1906. In 1920, women won the right to vote.

I spent my life fighting for equal rights. My dream came true.

What would you like to ask me?

1869

1820

Born 1820

1872

1920

Died 1906

glossary & index

glossary

abolitionist (ab-uh-LISH-uh-nist) someone who worked to end slavery before the Civil War

alcohol (AL-kuh-hawl) a drink like beer or wine

arrested (uh-REST-ed) stopped by the law

Quaker (KWAY-kur) a member of a Christian group; this group believes in peace and living a simple life

slavery (SLAY-vur-ee) a system where people own other people; slavery was legal in the United States until 1863

vote (VOHT) to pick a person to lead or a law to follow

index